Highland Dreams

Jamie MacSeaver

Copyright © 2017 by Jamie MacSeaver
All rights reserved. This book or any portion thereof
may not be reproduced or used in any manner whatsoever
without the express written permission of the publisher
except for the use of brief quotations in a book review.

Prologue

The screams of The Lady of McGregor, Annabel, were muted by the sound of bagpipes and tin whistles echoing in the hallways of the Estate House. A celebration had erupted when the Laird, Angus McGregor, announced his wife had gone into labour. All had believed her to be barren, yet after a long wait of six years, a child was on the way.

The whole estate was a frenzy, awaiting the baby's arrival.

"It's a wee baby boy!" The midwife gushed.

"Show me." Annabel whispered, tears in her eyes.

"Oh, I better tell Sir Angus! He'll be overjoyed. He's been dancing with the lads in the Great Hall since we started here." The senior maid said, clapping her hands.

"Aye, be careful though, Idelle. You're far along." Annabelle said, tired, eyeing Idelle's baby bump.

"Don't you worry, Miss. I'll be careful." Idelle smiled and departed.

She walked through the halls, searching for the Laird. She couldn't help skipping steps, the music bringing out her spirit. She found Angus, in the Great Hall and rushed to him.

"Sir, it's a boy!"

A deafening cheer erupted throughout the hall. An heir was here.

"Aye! But Idelle-"Angus started.

"Don't worry, Sir. The Lady is doing fine, she's tired only." Idelle assured him.

She left the men to their merry-making and went to tend to Lady Annabel. Idelle had been in their service since she was a young girl of only fifteen. She chuckled, thinking how coincidental it was for her and the Lady to be expecting together, although Idelle still had a few days to go. She entered the Lady's room just as the mid-wife was taking her leave.

"The Lady needs her rest and the baby needs proper care." The mid wife told Idelle.

"Aye, I'll make sure of it." Idelle told her.

Idelle moved to Annabel's bed side where the baby lay in his cradle.

"As handsome as his Da." Annabel croaked.

"Shh, Lady Annabel. You must rest." Idelle said, fluffing her pillows.

"As should you." Annabel said softly, smiling, before closing her eyes.

Idelle pulled the curtains close, giving her mistress some needed peace and quiet.

"Where is my boy?" Angus burst in, waking Annabel.

The baby cried at the sudden intrusion and his wails filled the room. Idelle picked him up to hush him as Angus went to his wife.

"My darling, how are you?" He asked her.

"I am fine, Angus. Don't ye worry." She told him as comfort.

The Laird was very fond of his wife, their marriage being one born out of youthful love. Angus kissed her forehead and turned to Idelle, who brought the baby over to him. He took his son in his arms.

"I name ye, Alpin. Alpin McGregor, heir to the McGregor's."

Idelle smiled, and left the room. Leaving man, wife and son to bond.

***

Idelle located her husband and found him, as usual, tending to the horses. He was the private coachman for the Laird and the Lady.

"There ye are." Idelle said.

Samuel looked up. A smile broke out on his face. Seeing the woman he loved carrying his child gave him a strange sense of pleasure.

"Aye. Idelle, ye shouldn't be walking so much." He said admonishingly. "Come sit, rest your legs."

Samuel finished his grooming work, and helped Idelle up. Together they made their way to their little cottage. Idelle felt stressed, the baby was kicking too much. A cold sweat broke out on her face. She clutched Samuel's arm, stopping him mid-step.

"I think ye better get the mid wife, dear." Idelle said, panting.

***

"It's a girl!" The mid wife exclaimed.

Idelle took her daughter in her arms, her breathing unbalanced. She had lost too much blood during the delivery.

The mid wife wiped the sweat off Idelle's forehead. She ushered Samuel in, who held his wife's hand tightly.

"I'll run out and get more help." The mid-wife said, running outside.

"We-we have to name her." Idelle said, unevenly. Her breathing was becoming shallower. "Isobel. I name ye Isobel."

"Don't ye close your eyes. They're coming." Samuel pleaded.

"Ye must vow to me, you'll love her for the both of us." Idelle said, her eyes closing.

"No, ye and I will love her together."

"Promise me, Samuel." Idelle begged, the darkness invading her sight.

"I promise." Samuel croaked out.

Idelle closed her eyes, unable to open them again. The celebrations in the Estate House continued while Samuel and little Isobel's wails echoed in the cottage, into the night.

***

Alpin grew up, spoilt reckless by his many admirers. Isobel grew up a fine version of her humble, responsible mother. The Lady had always respected Idelle, and took it upon herself to provide for Isobel as much as she could. Isobel spent her childhood learning how to sow and clean. She was destined to be a maid after all. Alpin grew up learning how to weave his sword and acquire land, a perfect son to the Laird and the clan.

Despite their societal status being different, Isobel and Alpin grew up playing together. She was his friend and he was hers. Every morning, as children, they would do whatever was required of them and then sneak out to meet in the gardens ready for another adventure.

They were nine years old now. Alpin was a spitting image of his father with the same black hair, cleft chin and tanned skin. Isobel, an exact replication of her late mother. Except for her hair, which was like her father's. Brown and curly, it hung down to her waist.

Isobel was in the garden, her face smeared with tears. Samuel had given her a scolding.

"Isobel! Look what I found." Alpin said, reaching her.

He opened his hands to show her a butterfly, and it flew away.

"That's nice." Isobel said, hiccupping.

"Why are ye crying, Isobel?" Alpin asked, worried about his best friend.

"Da says I shouldn't be friends with you. We're your servants."

"Nay, yer my best friend." Alpin said, "Ye and I are equal."

"Aye?"

"Aye. I will never ever let you go." Alpin said, and hugged her fiercely, causing both of them to fall down.

They lay on the grass, laughing and talking.

Years went by, and they grew up. As all children do. Their friendship intact and stronger than ever.

Chapter 1

Isobel woke early, as was her routine. She bathed herself and dressed. Alpin was gone on a hunting trip with his father. Isobel missed him and his cheerful presence. Having him around always made her happy. She was twenty-two years old now; a young virgin maiden. Her feelings for Alpin, starting out as friendship, had blossomed into young love. She loved him and he was unaware. Alpin still saw her as only a friend, a constant figure in his life.

However, he was returning today. Isobel was looking forward to seeing him. She had decided to let him know how she felt. As she had many time before. She would always decide to tell him, but looking at his handsome, clueless face, she'd weasel out. A fear resided in her heart, mingled with insecurities. No matter how strong a friendship they had, she was after all, and would always be, the daughter of servants. She, herself, was a maid now.

Today she was not backing down. Today is the day, Isobel thought, making her way to the Estate. Lady Annabel had asked her to prepare the Great Hall. The men would be returning soon and a feast would be held tonight. Her father had gone on the expedition with them. The Laird and the Lady were exceptionally kind and gracious towards them, never autocratic or imperious.

Isobel opened the curtains of the Great Hall to let in sunlight and fresh air. She dusted over the paintings and, with the help of her fellow maid and friend, Morag, mopped the floors. Morag had joined the service a year or so back, after her parents had died. The Laird, in order to help her survive, had given her a maid's post. Morag and Isobel had been friends ever since. Only she knew about Isobel's deepest desire; that is her love for Alpin.

"Morag, I'm doing it. Today." Isobel said, swinging her mop around.

"Aye, right." Morag said, rolling her eyes.

She had heard these words from Isobel more than once and to no avail.

"Ye numpty, I'm serious." Isobel said.

"I believe ye." Morag laughed.

The sound of the door opening, silenced them. Alpin walked in, striding angrily. Morag winked at Isobel, who scowled at her. She laughed quietly and left the room.

Alpin looked livid, his anger was raging. Isobel knew him well enough to know not to say anything now. He'd talk when he was ready. He paced around the hall, muttering under his breath. Isobel couldn't make out what it was but knew it was bad enough to upset him. Alpin rarely lost his temper. She took this time to admire him. His strong body and broad shoulders. His handsome face and black hair. She saved his eyes for last, knowing she'd lose herself in them. Yes, she would tell him how she felt.

"What are ye staring at?" Alpin said, snapping her out of her daze.

"Could ye be any ruder?" Isobel mocked.

Alpin relaxed his stance, apology in his eyes.

"I apologise." He said, before hugging her and swinging her around. "It's good to see ye."

"I barely noticed ye were absent." Isobel joked, before asking. "What are ye so barking mad for?"

"Trust me, it's absolutely right for me to be so enraged." Alpin said, pacing around her again. "Da, took me out in the woods to present me with an ultimatum."

"Which is…?"

"He believes that it is time for our clan to build a truce with neighbouring clans."

"Alpin, that be good news!" Isobel said.

She hushed when she saw his impatient expression.

"In order to do that, I am required to marry by the end of this coming summer. To a daughter of a Laird."

Isobel blinked back the tears as she realised what this meant. Bile rose in her throat as Alpin continued to ramble on. She had known this day would eventually come, yet she was not prepared. All thought of telling him her feelings left her head as she imagined Alpin in the arms of another woman. A stranger.

"Isobel, are ye even listening?" Alpin asked her.

"What?"

"Are ye alright. Yer as white as a ghost!" Alpin asked, making her sit.

"I, I'm fine. I didn't eat breakfast." She gave an excuse.

"Oh God, here I am barking about my problems." He said, as apology." Hold on, I'll get ye water and bread."

She tried to protest but shut up after seeing his expression. Alpin had always been over protective of her. She saw him leave from the entrance that led to the kitchen. She covered her face with her hands and broke down. She had deluded herself thinking they could have a future. She chastised herself for it, and pitied herself. A maid had no business falling in love with a future Laird. Fate was cruel. It was never meant to be.

***

Isobel stayed mute the remainder of the day until Morag finally asked,

"What is the matter with ye?"

"Nothing, Morag." Isobel said sullenly.

"Oh, spill the beans. What has ye in low spirits?" Morag insisted.

"Laird McGregor has decided it is time for Alpin to marry." She mumbled.

Morag understood what this meant for her friend. It meant her heart was breaking. She hugged Isobel as consolation and tried to distract her. The girls busied themselves with setting the feast. When the Great Hall was prepared, the family came down for dinner. Thy sat down and Alpin smiled at Isobel and Morag, who stood in the corner. Isobel couldn't muster up a smile and Alpin frowned, worried about her. He made to rise, but his father got up to make an announcement.

"Before ye start eating, I have an important announcement. I have received word from McLea, their Laird and his daughter will be visiting us in the morning. They'll be our guests and I expect everyone to be on their best behaviour." Laird McGregor said, eyeing Alpin.

Alpin was about to protest but Lady McGregor's look told him it was best not to. His father rarely ever changed his mind. Isobel felt despair. This visit meant one thing and one thing only. They come to seek a suitor.

Chapter 2

Isobel did not hover in the Great Hall longer than was required. She retreated to the kitchen, unable to hold back her tears. She felt silly for hoping for a future with Alpin. She truly loved him, he was the one since they were children. The one when who'd comfort her. The one who taught her how to protect herself. She smiled at the memory, them as teenagers, Alpin showing her how to use a knife. He had always looked out for her. She had fallen in love but he hadn't. It was fine, her love was strong enough for the both of them. She had been waiting and now there was no time left.

She knew it was no use to cry, it wouldn't help her feel better. She washed her face and prepared the bed warmers for the family. She knocked and entered the Laird and Lady's room. It was empty. Isobel put down the bed warmer, and moved to Alpin's room with a certain dread. Hoping it was empty, she knocked.

"Aye?" Alpin answered.

Isobel felt her shoulders slump. For the first time in her life she did not want to be around him. She walked in, planning to put the bed warmer and leave but he had other plans. As soon as Isobel placed the bed warmer, Alpin hugged her. He shook in anger, and Isobel couldn't help but hold him. It felt so perfect when they hugged, like an enigma coming together. His scent filled her nostrils, and she hid her face in his chest.

"Izzi, what do I do?" Alpin asked.

Isobel wish she knew how to help him. All she wanted was to scream out loud for him to love her and marry her. She opened her mouth but the words didn't come out.

"It's going to be alright, Alpin." Isobel finally said.

Alpin let go of her and started pacing.

"Nay, it won't be. It's not just the McLea. It's three clans altogether that I have to decide from." He scowled. "Ye decide for me. I trust ye know me best from all."

To her surprise, Isobel laughed. The idea of deciding a bride for the love of her life was amusing.

"What are ye laughing at, Rocket?" He snapped.

"I will not decide for ye. Yer on your own." Isobel, laughed.

In her laughter, she felt tears well up. She sobered and left quietly, ignoring Alpin's insistence. She couldn't be around him, discussing his future marriage.

***

The Lady McGregor had asked to see Isobel. Isobel found her in the garden, walking on her own.

"Ah, Isobel. There ye are." Lady McGregor said.

"Aye, My Lady. Ye asked for me?"

"Aye. The Laird and I think it's best if ye care for our guests for the time they are here. Specifically, Lavina, the daughter of the Laird of McLea." Lady McGregor told her.

"Of course, Miss." Isobel said.

Isobel hated the idea of it. The McLeas arrived within the hour after this conversation and the family welcomed them. The Laird of McLea looked to be a humble man but his daughter was anything but. Lavina was beautiful. One of the most beautiful girls Isobel had seen. However, she had a spoilt nature. Isobel hoped Alpin wouldn't be side-tracked by her beauty. Isobel led Lavina to the room she'd be staying in. The room was the best guest room in the whole Estate. Lady McGregor had made sure the finest was prepared to welcome her guests.

The moment Lavina walked in to it, her nose wrinkled.

"What is that ghastly smell?" She said snidely.

Isobel smelled nothing out of the ordinary and put the trunk next to her bed.

"Is there anything I can get for ye, Miss Lavina?"

"Another room would be nice. This is quite smaller than I'm used to."

Isobel looked around. The room was quite huge, enough for a family of three to live in quite comfortably.

"I'll see what I can do, Miss." Isobel told her, having no such intention.

Lavina moved to the bedside table and wiped a finger across it.

"Dust." She simply said.

Isobel had made sure the room was dusted and cleaned before bringing Lavina in. Lavina seemed to find faults in everything. She excused Isobel, who went downstairs to help prepare lunch. The chef had prepared the finest dishes for the lunch. Lavina came down in a beautiful dress, no doubt an expensive one. She sat opposite Alpin at the dinner table, batting her eyelashes at him coyly. Isobel snorted, quite loudly and everyone turned to look at her. She covered with a cough.

"Would ye like water?" Alpin offered her, getting up.

"I'm sure a servant will get her some." Lavina said.

Lavina did not know that Isobel and Alpin were best friends. He ignored her and brought over a flask of water for Isobel, much to Lavina's displeasure. The laird of McGregor and his family were exceptionally nice to their employees. Alpin would've done the same for anyone else.

"I wouldnae ride her in tae battle." He whispered, handing her the flask.

"Shh." Isobel scolded, hoping no one heard.

Alpin went back to the dinner table and sat down.

"We take very good care of our people." Alpin told Lavina, smiling sweetly.

Lavina smiled in return and Isobel saw the spite in her gaze. She was glaring at Isobel, and the Laird of McLea glared at his daughter. She had definitely failed to acquire Alpin's admiration. The remainder of the lunch was uneventful. Lavina tried to entice Alpin in to conversation, but he didn't respond the way she would've liked. Lavina was no doubt used to admiration, keeping in mind her looks, yet that did not win her any favours here. The McGregor's would never join hands with a clan if their people of higher power were spoilt, as Lavina was. The McGregor's, Isobel's clan, was one that was built on humility and focused on kinship. No matter what, Lavina would not be able to fit in.

There was hope after all.

Chapter 3

The McLeas were leaving. After lunch, father and daughter had disappeared into his room, and he emerged an hour later announcing their departure. Perhaps he had seen there wouldn't be any progress. Isobel had gone inside to help Lavina pack, and had seen that she was livid.

"Exit my room." Lavina snapped at her.

Isobel had left, as asked. She felt light-hearted for the first time in many days. They left right before dinner, not staying even when Lady McGregor insisted. Politely, in order not to offend them, Laird McGregor said he'd send word to them regarding their decision. It was mutually agreed, silently, that no such thing would occur. Isobel didn't stick around for dinner. Morag had said she could manage on her own. Tonight, Isobel would be dining with her father back at home. The moment she got home, she started on dinner preparation. Their work rarely allowed them to dine together and Isobel wanted to make it special.

Her father came in, tired as usual. From what she had heard, ever since her mother passed away, her father would busy himself with work until he could no longer go on. He'd come home, they'd talk for a while and then he would sleep. He had loved her mother, truly loved her. Losing her was too much for him. He loved Isobel too, but looking at her reminded him too much of his dear wife.

"Da, you need to take it easy." She admonished him.

"Nay, I'm fine." He reassured her.

They sat for dinner, a pleasant change.

"I heard the McLeas ran off." He winked at Isobel.

Although Isobel had never admitted it to him, sometimes she felt her father knew her feelings. Isobel hardly did a good job at hiding it. She blushed and ignored her father. He was her da, of course he knew. He had been in love once, too. He still was.

***

Isobel welcomed the morning in high spirits. She skipped down to the estate, greeting Morag.

"Yer awfully cheery?" Morag asked, happy in herself. "Could this be related to what the Laird said?"

Isobel was confused what she meant, her expression showed as much to Morag.

"Oh, aye. Ye weren't there." Morag said, "The Laird has said they won't be pursuing any clan. The right clan will come along on its own."

Isobel nearly jumped out of her shoes. The Laird was giving up his idea for Alpin marrying by the end of summer.

"That's a good decision." Isobel said diplomatically. She couldn't hide her glee and nearly jumped on Morag, giggling animatedly.

"Alright, ye roaster." Morag calmed her, "Go get some water from the well."

Isobel set off with the buckets in hand. She was drawing water when she heard someone panting behind her. She turned around and her brain functionality halted. Alpin stood against the wall, shirtless, only in his trews. Sweat covered his chest and his lower abdomen, the sun light glinting off it, making it shine. Isobel could not focus on her task.

It never bothered Alpin to be half-dressed around Isobel. He had no idea the way he beguiled her.

"Been looking everywhere for ye. It's so hard to track ye." He said, breathing heavily, "I just finished sparring, give me some water."

Isobel filled a bucket and brought it over to him. He spilled the bucket over his head and shook it off.

"Ah, that's better." He said, refreshed.

"I'm glad." Isobel grinned.

"I'm glad to be rid of that minx Lavina." Alpin said.

"Oh, that's a bit too much." Isobel said, secretly pleased.

"Oh, come off it. She was a misery." Alpin said, and then mimicked Lavina, "I'm queen of the kingdom."

Isobel laughed and Alpin joined in. Alpin noticed the knife that hung from Isobel's belt. He had gifted it to her.

"Ye still carry that?"

"Of course, need to protect myself." Isobel joked.

She knew she carried it as a souvenir of his friendship.

"Ye still remember what I taught ye?" Alpin asked her.

"Aye." Isobel said proudly.

"Confident, are we?" Alpin asked, drawing his knife.

Isobel drew hers and the two practiced their skills. Alpin was pleased; she remembered well. They practiced for a little while and soon tired. Isobel lay on the floor and Alpin lay beside her as they used to in their childhood.

"Ye remember well." Alpin said.

"I told ye so." Isobel said cockily.

Alpin turned, facing her. They were lying closer than usual.

"Yer the only woman in my life to understand me as ye do." He said honestly.

This felt real. Isobel wanted nothing more than to tell him how she felt, to tell him the truth. It would make things so much easier. Isobel was debating over it when Alpin continued,

"It would be a lot easier if there was a woman like you. I'd marry her." He joked.

Isobel felt hurt. He really didn't love her. He'd marry someone like her but never her. She swallowed back the tears and got up. Alpin followed.

"Want to practice some more?" He offered.

"Nay, I have work." Isobel told him quietly, and went to draw water.

Alpin felt confused. Had he said something wrong?

"I'll see you later then." He murmured as Isobel walked away with the water.

She didn't look back. She had been foolish to feel hopeful. So what if Laird McGregor had given up his idea? It did not mean that Alpin would fall in love with her. He had never seen her that way, and would never. She was just a friend. Friends don't fall in love with friends. The same friend whose family they serve. The same friends who were out of their league by status. Friends they had no business falling in love with.

Isobel decided to ignore her love, her friend for days to come. She focused on doing what she did best, serving the family; a maid's tale.

Chapter 4

A week had since passed. Alpin had noticed how Isobel had withdrawn from him. No matter how much he tried to engage her in conversation, she wouldn't respond as well as she used to. Alpin could not figure out the cause for the rift that had come between them. He asked Morag one day when she came to place his bed warmer. As of late, Morag had taken over Isobel's nightly duty.

"Morag, Is there something the matter with Isobel?" He asked her.

"No, Sir." Morag answered, looking away.

She bowed and left, leaving Alpin contemplating.

***

"He asked about ye." Morag said, coming to the foyer.

"Oh." Isobel said simply.

"Ye could go see him." Morag said.

"Aye." Isobel said. "But there is no need for it."

A knock on the main door attracted their attention. It was almost midnight, a late hour for any visitors.

"Probably a beggar." Morag said.

Isobel went to the door and unlocked it. A woman stood, her back to them, and turned around at the door opening. She had red hair, curly and untamed. Her eyes were wild and lively, her face fierce. She carried a bow and a sword. From afar, she looked like a true warrior. Her aura projected confidence. She walked in without hesitation.

"I am Aisla. Daughter of The Laird of Campbell." She announced.

Isobel ran after her and threw a worried glance at Morag.

"Please alert the Laird of my arrival." Aisla motioned to Morag, who scurried off leaving Isobel alone with her.

As was protocol, Isobel led her to the Great Hall. After making sure she was comfortable, Isobel checked the hallways to see if Morag was back. She was nowhere to be seen. Aisla had no doubt come back from a hunting trip. A scar glistened on her face, fresh with blood.

'May I get you an ointment and some tea?" Isobel asked, politely.

"Aye." Aisla told her, checking her bow.

Isobel fixed a tray with warm milk, tea and sugar. She sliced a loaf of bread, and put it on the tray along with the ointment. She picked it up and went back to the Great Hall. The Laird was talking with Aisla. They were laughing.

"Aye, good lassie Isobel. Please prepare a bed for Miss. Campbell." Laird McGregor told her.

Isobel served them tea and went to do as instructed. Morag followed her, no doubt to discuss why the girl had arrived unannounced.

"It's a wee bit odd, don't ye think?" Morag asked Isobel. "Coming when the sky is black as the Earl of Hell's Waistcoat!"

"Haud yer wheesht! Someone will hear." Isobel said. "It is quite odd though. Perhaps we were near to where she was hunting."

"Bit mad for a girl to be out on her own for hunting."

"It's not our business either way." Isobel said, ending the conversation.

***

Isobel entered the Great Hall the following morning to find Alpin and Aisla engrossed in conversation. They were laughing, the sound echoing off the walls. His fascination with her was quite apparent. Isobel had never seen him holding onto someone's words so fiercely. Alpin saw Isobel walk in. She helped Morag serve breakfast. When she was about to leave, Alpin stopped her.

"Isobel, listen to this." Alpin told her, "Aisla went to hunt wild boar. ON HER OWN."

It seemed like a big deal to him, but Isobel couldn't care less. She smiled politely, without interest.

"Aye, three. They were feisty but no match for my sword." Aisla announced proudly.

The Laird and Lady were passing approving looks, eyeing the gross fascination their son had for Aisla. She had the whole family wrapped around her finger. Isobel could see there was no place for her in this setting. She stayed, listening to Aisla joke and entertain the family. When she couldn't pretend to be happy any longer, she went back to work.

At noon, Lady Mcgregor came looking for Alpin and found Isobel instead.

"Have you seen Alpin, Isobel?" She asked.

"No, My Lady." Isobel told her.

She hadn't seen Alpin since breakfast in the morning, where he was enraptured by Aisla.

"Can ye please seek him and ask him to come meet me. The Laird and I have to discuss something with him."

"Aye." Isobel told her, and went looking for him.

He was nowhere to be found in the Estate. In fact, Aisla wasn't either. No doubt they were together and talking about their different styles of hunting, Isobel thought snidely. It made her envious that Alpin found her so charming. Isobel agreed with Morag, it was too strange for Aisla to show up out of the blue.

Isobel went to the lower bailey, hoping he was there. She could heart grunts and the sound of metal clinking. She found him and Aisla. Much to her chagrin, Isobel saw that Alpin was teaching her how to use a pocket knife. They quit when Isobel entered. Both panting heavily.

"The Laird and Lady are asking for ye, Alpin." Isobel said formally.

"I'm fair puckled!" Alpin guhes, "Ye are one fine fighter."

Aisla blushed as Alpin looked at her. Isobel felt like she could puke.

"Haste Ye Back!" Aisla said, as Alpin went to answer his parents.

Aisla picked up her kerchief and wiped the sweat off her face. She winged her sword around, practicing her moves. Isobel looked at her with envy. Aisla was turning out to be more and more of a perfect match for Alpin. Alpin had said Isobel was the only woman who understood him. That wasn't the case anymore. Isobel left Aisla to her practice. Her sorcery had already worked its magic. She had taken Isobel's place in Alpin's life.

***

Isobel was sorting out the books in the study when Alpin came in. He looked thrilled, the conversation with his parents had gone well.

"I'm marrying her. I'm going to ask her father for her hand." He nearly shouted.

Isobel dropped the books in her hand and scrambled to pick them up.

"That's great." She said, feeling anything but.

"Aye. Have ye seen Aisla?" He asked.

"Nay." She told him.

"Find her. No, wait." He changed his mind, "Da thinks I shouldn't discuss it with her until I have her father's approval."

"I suppose." Isobel said.

She could not bring herself to be happy for him.

"I can't believe I'm in love." Alpin gushed.

Isobel snapped her head up. Love? He loved her? Already? Her heart broke hearing this. Isobel smiled for his sake. She broke down when he left. What had she gotten herself into? She wiped her tears and resolved to stop caring. It would help her forget him. For he did not belong to her anymore. He never did.

Chapter 5

Aisla had been here for two days, with no intention of leaving any time soon. Alpin and she spent most of their time together these days. Isobel tried to avoid any confrontations with them, whatsoever. She had vigorously been cleaning the rooms that had been closed for as long as she remembered. She had taken permission from Lady McGregor and was deep cleaning the old rooms.

The rooms were a site of fascination for anyone who appreciated souvenirs and relics. No one came in here or was allowed to, in case they'd steal anything. These rooms held the history of her land and clan. Today she was going to clean the room with the most expensive of artefacts. She went to the door and it was open already. That's strange, Isobel thought before going inside.

Aisla stood in the room, her back to Isobel. The sound of footsteps made her turn around.

"Oh, I lost my way. I'm looking for the study." She told Isobel, flustered.

"It's down the hall. On the other side of the estate." Isobel told her coolly.

Aisla quickly left, her head down and hands closed in front of her. Isobel wondered if she should inform anyone of Aisla's presence in this room. She decided she should tell Alpin, and remembered how smitten he was with Aisla. It would only cause them to argue. Besides, what business did Isobel have questioning someone of Aisla's status? She thought it better to just keep her head down and mind her own business.

Isobel finished cleaning the room and left, closing the door behind her. She forgot about the incident with Aisla until Morag told her that she had left. Something was amiss. It was worrisome that Aisla had left during the short span of the time it took Isobel to clean that room. Could it be related to what she had seen?

Morag told her that Aisla had left saying she had to go hunting and would return a week later. It all seemed pretentious to Isobel. Deciding it was her duty to inform Alpin of this, she slept waiting for the morning to tell him. She also resolved to finally admit her feelings for him. A mental frenzy had taken over her. She felt courage. Seeing Alpin with Aisla had made her realize just how shattered she'd be if he married someone else. She did not care if he did not reciprocate. She had to tell him.

She hurriedly dressed in the morning, eager to go meet Alpin. She didn't find him in the Great Hall at breakfast and went to check his room. It was empty and she felt her nerves rise. She rushed downstairs, and went to Morag.

"Where is he? Alpin." She said, worried. "Have ye seen him?"

"Nay. Isobel, are ye okay?" She asked, concerned.

"Nay." Isobel said and left.

She searched the grounds with no signs of him. She finally went to the stable. Her father was tending to the horses when she reached them.

"Da, have ye seen Alpin?" She asked him.

"Aye, early in the morning. He left to go to Campbell lands. Something about askin for a girl's hand." Her father told her.

Isobel caught up and panicked. She had taken too long. He was on his way to ask her father already. Realising she had no more time left to lose, Isobel got up on the closest horse.

"What are ye doing, ye roaster?" Her father scolded.

Isobel didn't listen to him and pulled the reigns, making the horse move forward. The horse galloped and Isobel screamed back,

"I have to ge after him! I have to tell him I love him, Da!"

Samuel smiled. His daughter had found her courage. He watched his daughter race against the wind, her horse racing her forward in search of her love. She was every bit as brave and fierce as her mother. The love of Samuel's life.

***

Isobel was lost. She had never been this far from home. She had only been to the outskirts on a few occasions, accompanied by her father or Alpin. The thought of Alpin made her go forward, stubborn as she was. They had been on the right track until a snake startled her horse and it ran off in the opposite direction of the right way. Fear that he was already halfway to the Campbell Clan made her anxious. For the first time, Isobel had found the courage to seek him out and tell him the truth. And he had disappeared before she could.

More than that, she wanted to tell him about the peculiar incident with Aisla before she had disappeared. It was a cause of worry. Isobel wandered on her horse in different directions. There was no one around for miles but woods and woods. The sun would set in a few hours, and in the darkness Isobel would have no chance of finding Alpin.

"Alpin!" Isobel screamed.

No answer came back. She tried again,

"ALPIN!"

A movement caught her attention and she looked around. She could see figures moving behind the trees and her breath caught. Alpin hadn't found her, but nomads had. She tried to get control of her horse but it was as scared as her. Four men came forward, dressed in torn kilts with patches of cloth sewn on them. Isobel knew they would try to grab her and capture her for ransom. She withdrew her knife, ready to defend herself.

"A knife?" One of the nomads asked, laughing. "Yer gonna need more than one, Missy."

He made to grab Isobel and she slashed her knife across her throat. He fell on the ground clutching his neck that bled out. The motion startled her horse and it dropped her and ran off. The remaining three nomads grabbed Isobel. She had managed to slice the first one so he lay dead on the ground. This did not please the others and they bound her in ropes and carried her off.

"ALPIN!" Isobel shouted, before they put a ball of cloth in her mouth to silence her.

Chapter 6

They had thrown Isobel on the ground of their camping site, harshly. A fire crackled in front of Isobel, and she noticed her surroundings. They were in a deeper part of the forest now. No one could locate them here. She felt foolish for screaming out Alpin's name so often. No doubt, they had heard and found her. Nomadic thieves were a nuisance in many parts of the unclaimed lands.

They stood in deep discussion, and Isobel wondered what they would do with her. They would kill her, or worse rape her and leave her in the woods to die. She couldn't let them, she had to get out of here. They had taken her knife and she had no way to free herself from the ropes. Isobel started struggling on the ground to free herself.

One of the nomads came towards her and took the cloth from her mouth.

"Quit foolin' around, ye walloper!" He said sternly.

"LET ME GO! ALPIN!" Isobel screamed.

The man put the cloth back in her mouth.

"Shut ye geggie!" He screamed back.

"Quit shouting ye oaf!" Another man told him.

"Who gets the first go?" The third man asked.

The hair on Isobel neck's rose, and cold sweat broke out on her face. Rape it was. Tears stung her eyes and she begged God to send her father, Alpin or anyone to save her. The man who had screamed at her, pulled her up and started to undo the ropes. Isobel shook, feeling dizzy. She wanted to throw up.

A scurry of movement behind Isobel stopped the man. He moved back.

"Who's there? Show yerself." He asked to the darkness.

"Let the girl go and step back." Alpin's voice came from behind her.

Isobel turned around and gasped. He was here and he looked scary. She ran to him.

"Alpin." She said through sobs.

"Shh, I'm here." He soothed her, wrapping one arm around her. The other held his sword, ready to strike.

"Yer off yer head, taking what's ours." A nomad told him.

They picked up their swords. Alpin handed his pocket knife to Isobel. A nomad tried to grab her and Alpin swashed the sword across his arm, cutting it off. The man howled in pain as the other two hesitated. Isobel readied herself to defend, her knife facing forward. The remaining nomads made for Alpin, to defeat the stronger of the two. Alpin engaged with one and Isobel tried to distract the other. She used all the tricks and skills Alpin taught her, she kicked the man in the shin, and stabbed him with her knife. He fell. Alpin had managed to tackle the other man on his own and he too lay panting on the floor, blood gushing from many wounds.

"Gather their swords." Alpin barked at Isobel.

He was infuriated. Isobel was scared and did as he instructed. They bound the nomads with the same ropes they had used on Isobel. Alpin took her hand and ran through the woods to where his horse stood waiting.

"If ye hadn't come- "Isobel started and broke down.

"Are ye barking mad? What are ye doing here?!" He roared at Isobel.

"I-"

"What would give ye the idea of following me around? Have ye no brains on ye?" He said angrily.

Isobel felt scared and said the first thing that came to her mind.

"The Laird. Your da asked me to." She said.

Alpin was confused. Why would his father have him followed?

"Why-"

"To accompany ye. Make sure their family is well matched for yers." Isobel muttered, looking away from him.

Alpin felt bad for screaming at her. His expression softened and he hugged her.

"Forgive me. I was too harsh." He started "If anything had happened to ye-"

"It's okay, I'm fine." Isobel said, accepting his apology.

They stood hugging for a while, comforting each other. The moonlight fell upon them from the small spaces through the trees. Isobel felt a swell of emotion as Alpin clutched her close to his chest. She felt tears well up and sobbed.

"Hey, I am truly sorry, ye roaster." He joked.

"I should've been more careful." Isobel said, feeling ashamed.

"Nay, Ye did well. A true warrior." Alpin said. "My father should've sent someone with ye. But I'm glad ye can be here with me."

He still felt confused as to why his father would not trust him enough to judge the Campbells. Yet he felt an odd sense of composure now that Isobel was here. She was his best friend and he was glad he was taking this important decision with her by his side.

Isobel, however, felt shame and guilt for lying to him. How could she tell him she had lied and come at her own decision? He would be infuriated at her for taking the risk. But she had to. If Alpin was going to ask for Aisla's hand in marriage and wed her, she had to let him know how she felt. After that, she would let him go. Never look back. Isobel understood how important this marriage would be for their clan, an important pact with the Campbells. A maid and coachman's daughter could not bring the clan such an advantage.

She would tell him soon, and resign to being just his ally, his friend.

"Let's build a small fire and camp till the sun rises. Ye should rest." Alpin added.

"Aye." Isobel said, lost in her thoughts.

Chapter 7

A small fire crackled in between Alpin and Isobel. Both lay on mats on the ground, looking upwards at the beautiful sky. The silence between them was comfortable, intense. They had grown up together and rarely found themselves feeling awkward at the quiet.

"It's mesmerizing." Alpin said, looking at the sky and turning towards her. "Covered with stars all around."

"It really is." Isobel said, facing him.

"Remember how ye and I would sneak out after hours." Alpin said. "We'd look at the sky for hours on end."

"Of course I remember. I also remember the beating my da gave when he found out." Isobel laughed. "Running out in the middle of the night to look at stars!"

Alpin laughed.

"You'd always come back the next night." Alpin said, smiling. "Nothing kept you away. My only friend."

Isobel felt nostalgic, remembering the times when it was only Alpin and her against the world. Two children. She almost spilled her heart out, but knew better. He loved someone else now, more than he ever loved her.

"Ye have more friends now." Isobel said, hiding her sadness.

"Who?" Alpin asked, incredulous

"Aisla." Isobel said.

"Aisla? She's not a friend. She's something else." Alpin said, folding his arms under his head.

"She's the one ye love." Isobel mused.

"I do. She's different. She's- "

"Amazing, I know." Isobel said, rolling her eyes.

"Not only that. She has a strong aura that draws me to her. So fierce, so quirky." He sighed, his infatuation evident.

So secretive, Isobel thought silently. Alpin was infatuated with her, without knowing much about her or her past. Isobel could not let her friend make such a big mistake. She decided to tell him what she had seen. Putting aside her own feelings, she knew regardless he was making a mistake thinking he loved her without knowing her.

He loved whatever Aisla had portrayed to him. An image of himself, in a woman.

"Alpin, I saw something." Isobel started, "With Aisla, I mean."

"Aye?" Alpin asked, confused. "What did ye see?"

"She was in the old rooms when I was in there cleaning." She said slowly. "She panicked when she saw me and left."

"Oh. That's no cause for worry. Relax, Isobel." Alpin said, nonchalantly. "She was only looking around."

Isobel felt her aggravation rise.

"How blinded are ye by her?" Isobel snapped. "She wasn't looking around, she was lurking. Ye know no one can enter the old castle."

Alpin froze, shocked at the venom in her voice.

"Isobel." He said sternly.

"Nay, she was in the forbidden corridors!" Isobel nearly shouted.

"As were ye!" Alpin snapped, matching her anger.

Isobel did not bother replying, hurt that he'd doubt her. Her from all people. Doubt her over his precious Aisla. Isobel had lived there her entire life, he knew better than to think she was up to no good. She also knew he did not mean it in that way, but couldn't care less in her envy and fury.

"Look, that came out wrong." Alpin started.

"Don't bother, Master Alpin. I only wished to inform my employers and I have." She said cordially. "What do I have to gain from meddling in your business and protecting your family?"

"Isobel!" Alpin scolded.

She didn't bother replying, turning her head away from him and closing her eyes. After a few moments, Alpin turned around too. If she wanted to be a child, so be it, Alpin thought. Yet, he had upset her and could not simply sleep. He stayed awake for a long time until a small sob reached his ears. She too was unable to sleep. He sighed and turned around again.

"Izzie, I didn't mean it like that." He reasoned with her. "I merely meant there's no reason to be so suspicious."

"Don't bother yerself. I expect nothing more from a boy who is smitten with a girl he met only a few days ago and with whom he already claims to be in love." Isobel said, not turning towards him. He could hear the seriousness in her voice through her tears. He wondered if she was right, but paid no attention to it. Of course he loved Aisla. He knows his heart. But he could also feel his heart reanalysing and deliberating, so he pushed the thought away. For now, he was hurt by the way Isobel was treating him.

"Smitten? I love her, Isobel." He said, forcefully.

"I wonder who you're trying to convince. Yerself or me?" She said hollowly.

Isobel wanted to break down and tell him there and then that she loved him. His defensive attitude and insistence on what he believed to be true had maddened her and she did not care anymore for what he said. If he wanted to put this noose around his neck, Isobel could not stop him. She was definitely not going to stand by and watch as Aisla tightened it. Isobel had almost run out of time though. They were a day or two away from the Campbell settlement. Her heart sank and she fell into slumber, dreaming of a life where Aisla didn't exist and Alpin was hers.

***

The sun was coming up and the light was too much to stay asleep any longer. Isobel rubbed her eyes and stretched on the mat, turning over and realising she was on the ground and not on her bed. She got up with a start, and sat, remembering the events of last night. The nomads, the fight and her argument with Alpin. He was still asleep, his arm covering his eyes from the sun. She felt a surge of emotion, love, hate, anger and happiness. One human alone had the capability to bring forth so much from within her.

She looked at him sleeping, admiring his face and physique. She wanted to reach out with her hand and cradle him in her arms. She hesitated and then got up and walked away. Wanting to clear her head. The longer he slept, the more time they had left together before Aisla forever replaced her.

Chapter 8

"We're a day or a bit more away now." Alpin said, putting the saddle on his horse. Isobel was putting out the fire. Alpin had woken up an hour or so ago and, without wasting time, had started preparing for departure for the Campbells. He and Isobel weren't talking beyond what was necessary to communicate important things. The previous night's fight was still fresh, hanging like a loose nail between them, ready to drop.

Isobel did not try to make amends and neither did Alpin. Both were right in their anger, according to them and wanted an apology from the other. Alpin got on his horse and offered his hand to Isobel. She refused to take it and got on the horse unaided, albeit with some difficulty. They left the clearing as the sun was out completely, showering its rays on the highlands. They rode on clear land, the woods running next to them.

Isobel had her arms around his waist, to prevent her from falling as the horse moved ahead. Apart from that they made no contact. They rode for a little while at a steady slow pace. Isobel scoffed, wondering why he wasn't rushing to his bride. Alpin was lost in his own thoughts, remembering what she had said last night. He heard her murmuring behind him, and decided to break the ice.

"What's that?" he asked, his gaze set forward, intently staring at the land.

"Nothing, Sir." Isobel said, her voice piercingly cold.

Silence.

"Lady Isobel, what are ye thinking?" Alpin said, light heartedly. He was trying to erase the tension that gnawed between them.

"Nothing that concern ye, Master Alpin." Isobel said, monotonously.

Silence again. Alpin did not bother to make amends after that. They were riding closer to the woods now, the path shifting towards them. A deer ran out from the woods and nearly collided with their horse. Seeing the deer, the horse bolted and Alpin nearly lost his grip on the reigns. Isobel fell off the horse, and after calming it down, Alpin got off to help her. The deer stared at them and grunted. He was lost and searching for his herd.

Isobel took the hand Alpin offered and got up off the ground. She dusted the soil from her dress and looked at the deer. He grunted again and ran back into the woods. Isobel raced after him, grabbing Alpin's bow and arrow off the horse as she went. Alpin had taught her to hunt long ago when they were children. Before she had matured, The Laird would permit little Isobel to accompany their hunting party, for she was not used to being away from her father for too long. On those wild trips, she had picked up the art with Alpin's assistance.

Alpin caught up on her intention and raced after her with his dagger. They were going to hunt that deer, like old times. They entered the woods cautiously, so as to not scare the deer off. It was walking slower now, safe in the woods. Alpin saw that Isobel had the bow in her arm, ready to launch the arrow when the deer stopped. She had a few skills practiced and he knew she couldn't hunt the deer as long as it was not mobile. The deer was unaware of the hunter ready to strike. It stopped next to a small puddle to quench its thirst and Alpin saw Isobel take a deep breath before she released the arrow. Alpin took a step forward slowly, but his foot stepped onto dry leaves, the sound echoing.

The deer turned and ran again. Isobel's gaze followed him and so did the arrow. She turned around, her eyes following the deer and she launched the arrow. It struck the deer on its neck and it fell on the ground, struggling to get up. Isobel got off the rock she stood on and ran to the deer as Alpin watched in admiration. Her technique had improved sufficiently over time. He approached her and the deer that was still flaying its legs and arms.

"Get yer dagger, Alpin." Isobel said, impressed with herself for hitting her target perfectly.

Alpin got down and sat next to her on the ground. He rubbed his hand on the deer's body, trying to soothe its pain. He lifted his dagger from its belt and passed it to Isobel.

"Ye do it." She said, shifting the deer's head in the right position. Alpin slit its throat, ending its misery. He flayed his legs one last time and stopped.

"Yer technique has gotten better." Alpin complimented her, wiping his dagger on the deer's skin and putting it back in his belt.

"I suppose. I had a great teacher, ye see." Isobel said, her anger vanished.

"Is that a compliment?" Alpin asked in mock horror. Isobel pushed him, and he tripped.

"Could ye be any more annoying?" Isobel snapped at him, jokingly.

Alpin stared at the fresh mud on his clothes and looked at her with determination. Isobel knew what he was going to do. She started retreating.

"Don't ye dare. I'm warning ye." Isobel said, her voice serious. She took a few more steps and tripped on a rock, falling down. Her dress was covered in mud, like his, smeared together with the deer's blood.

Alpin roared in laughter, the sound cascading off the tree barks, into their surroundings. Isobel got up and shook her hands to rid them of the mud. Her eyes were bloody murder as she stared at him, wanting revenge.

"Ye oaf! Look what ye did! YOU MADE ME FALL!" She screamed at him, only encouraging his laughter to escalate.

"ME? Yer the one walking backwards like numpty." He choked out through tears of pure glee.

Isobel was not letting him off the hook for this so easily. She bent and gathered a handful of mud; Alpin knew what she was doing. Before she could throw it at him, Alpin turned on his heels and ran away from her. Isobel ran after him, screaming,

"I'm going to get ye for this! Just watch!" Isobel said loudly.

Alpin laughed even harder at her indignation and continued to run.

"I'm so scared!" Alpin said, his voice dripping humour and sarcasm.

They ran out the woods, into the clearing where the horse waited. Isobel was close enough for Alpin to grab when she stumbled on her dress and fell forward. Alpin caught her and they fell together. Together, they rolled down the clearing that sloped downwards, their laughter and screams loudly resonating. They slowed down and tumbled to a stop, both breathless.

"Look what ye did!" Alpin said, chuckling. His face was red and his eyes were fiery.

"Oh shut up!" Isobel gushed, blushing due to his close proximity. They were on the ground in each other's arms, entangled together. They lay panting for a while, until they sobered up.

"I'm sorry." Alpin said, wanting the argument to end. He did not understand why but whenever he and Isobel fought, his heart felt empty as if there was a crucial part of it missing. He couldn't decipher what it was and the depth of this emotion. He only knew he had to fix it.

"I am as well. Truce?" Isobel asked. She knew she couldn't let their friendship end over Aisla, no matter how much her presence plagued this relationship.

"Aye." Alpin said, getting off the ground and helping her up.

"Onwards to Campbell?" Isobel asked, unsure.

Alpin stared in the direction they were to head to reach Campbell. He felt conflicted, and stared back and forth between Isobel and the way. After a minute, he went towards the horse and got on.

"Aye." He said flatly.

Together, they resumed their journey. They'd mended their friendship, and that's all that mattered to Isobel. She could sacrifice her love for his happiness, no matter with whom he sought it. However, Alpin wondered why he thought of Isobel as the most intriguing woman in his life, and not Aisla. He hadn't thought of his future wife once during the course of the hunt. What bothered him most was that he had forgotten all about her for those few minutes.

Chapter 9

Farther along from the woods where they had hunted down the deer, they came across a campsite. It lay a mile away from them, and they could see the tents set up and people walking here and there. A hunting party. Isobel wondered who they were as they neared. It could be a civilized bunch of nomads, which was a rarity. Or another clan. They were closer now and Isobel could see their tartan colours embellished on the flag pitched into the soil, flowing with the wind.

The flag was blue, black and red. Isobel had never seen it before, but obviously Alpin had.

"Oh nay." Alpin said, as they stopped right outside the entrance to the small settlement.

"Ye know them?" Isobel mused, craning her neck to get a better look.

"The Sutherlands." Alpin said, his voice resigned. "This won't be too good."

A man approached them, dressed in hunting attire.

"Hello, we're just passing by." Alpin said. Isobel noticed his hesitance to communicate more than was necessary. Perhaps their clan did not get along with the Sutherlands.

"Hello! Good day to ye, laddie!" The man said, cheerfully. He looked at Alpin and Isobel, no doubt noticing the colours they wore. "Hold on! You're a McGregor! Are ye Master Alpin??"

A look of recognition took its place on the man's face and he ushered their horse forward, not taking a no for an answer.

"Aye but we really can't stop, we're on a tight schedule." Alpin tried reasoning. He really did not want to be here.

"Oh Alpin, why are ye saying no to warm food and shelter? I'm hungry and tired!" Isobel whispered to him.

"Shush!" Alpin admonished her. She did not understand the stakes at risk.

"We really must leave." Alpin tried again. The man had already led their horse into the settlement.

"Nonsense! The Laird will be displeased with me if I let his son-in-law leave without having them meet!" The man chuckled.

Isobel's blood became cold, her heart raced. The Sutherlands were one of the clans that Laird McGregor had approached for marriage to Alpin. This is why the man was so eager to have Alpin stay. He wanted to please him and impress him. Isobel felt her spirits drop, the happiness that had engulfed her evaporated.

***

Alpin was pacing in the tent they had been given. Isobel sat on the sleeping mat and watched him calculating something in his head. Isobel, although depressed did not see any reason for him to be reacting in this way.

"Why are ye pacing? Not happy to meet the in laws?" Isobel asked, her voice sarcastic.

Alpin rolled his eyes at her and continued thinking. He stopped for a second and then started pacing again and stopped.

"The Sutherlands can bring the most to our clan with this union and gain quite a lot in return. They are unaware that I have chosen Aisla, and are under the impression that we are still seeking a suitor." Alpin said slowly, expressing his conflict. "I believe they were on their way to our lands, after this hunting trip ended."

"Oh." Isobel said, tonelessly. She had lost all hope ever since Alpin had chosen Aisla.

This did not affect her as much as it would've before. She only worried for the relations her clan had with the Sutherlands.

"I'm thinking of a way to leave without mentioning where we are headed. I'd prefer if Da talks to them about the decision we've made. It'll be better if it comes from an elder of our clan." He mused, asking for her insight.

"I suppose that makes sense. Ye can be this far out for hunting yerself." Isobel agreed, "I don't think it'll be evident. Your true reasons for travelling."

"Yer right. Aye, it can work." Alpin said as a man entered their tent. He wore a wolf skin coat, his body buff and strong. He was quite large and walked with a proud posture.

"Hello, I am Laird Sutherland!" He boasted, shaking Alpin's hand with a firm grip. "Ye came out to seek us yerself? We were on way to your side of the area, anyhow."

"Nay, we were actually out hunting ourselves." Alpin clarified.

"We?" The Laird asked, and looked at Isobel, noticing her presence in the room.

"Aye, my friend Lady Isobel and myself." Alpin smiled.

Isobel took a bow and greeted the laird, who was not smiling any longer.

"Son, I hardly understand the need to be out so far from home, hunting with a girl." The Laird said, eyeing Isobel with clear judgement in his gaze. Isobel felt that he intended to belittle her, and hung her head.

"I'm afraid I don't understand what ye mean, Laird." Alpin asked, offended by the remark.

"Why, ye are to be married, with my daughter no less. I don't see it suitable for ye to be tittle tallying with another girl." The Laird said, his voice rising slightly.

"Sir, with all due respect, I am as yet not married to yer daughter and we have made no such promise to ye." Alpin snapped, forgetting his manners.

"How dare ye! Yer father has asked us to meet ye, we did not approach ye." The Laird said, clarifying that he did not need them. "My daughter is not lacking in suitors."

"I'm sure then it won't be a problem if I pull myself out of the race, sir." Alpin said, cordially.

"What is the meaning of this?" The Laird asked angrily.

"I am actually on my way to the Campbells." Alpin said. It wouldn't take the Laird too long to figure out what this meant.

"Nonsense! Ye are insulting me, Master McGregor. It won't take me long to send news to the Campbells ye are frolicking with another girl out in the woods, away from the public eye!" The Laird said snidely.

Isobel felt insulted and blushed red with anger. He was outright calling her an immoral woman. It enraged Alpin more than it did her. He couldn't let his friend be insulted like this because of his fault.

"I will ask ye to be a bit more respectful, sir. Ye are accusing us of immoral deeds which we have not committed!" Alpin snarled, standing straighter.

"I will not allow a foolish, disrespectful boy to address me this way within the confines of my own settlement!" The Laird's anger was obvious and Isobel feared he'd hurt Alpin. She tried to move forward to stop Alpin from answering. She was too late.

"And I will not allow a self-righteous Laird to insult me and my friend. Now, we'll be leaving before ye can spite some more horrifying comments." Alpin said. He picked up his dagger and motioned Isobel towards the exit.

"Yer father will be hearing of this! I will make sure of it!!" The Laird shouted, following them out. Alpin quietly led Isobel to their horse and they mounted.

"I'm sure he'll understand who's at fault." Alpin said, and pulled the reigns of the horse. They galloped out of the campsite, Isobel's heart still racing.

"Alpin, that won't be the end of it. They'll create trouble and fights! He was insulted." Isobel said, her voice barely audible over the wind.

"Aye. I know. Best we can hope is we reach Campbell before their message does." Alpin roared, so she could hear him.

"Ye know this will cause tension amongst the Lairds." Isobel told him as a warning.

"Aye, what can I say? They all want me to marry their daughters." Alpin said cockily and chuckled. Isobel smiled, unconvincingly. She was anything but happy about that. It only made her mentally manic, to reveal her feelings to him. She couldn't hold it back anymore.

Chapter 10

Alpin and Isobel had left the Sutherland campsite way behind them. She was worried what impact the incident at the campsite would have. Alpin however had another incident on his mind altogether. He was thinking about Isobel. Her ferocity, the way she had brought down the deer, with such precision and skill. He always admired that about her, her strong command over her mind and body. He thought about how they had tumbled down the slope, arms and legs intertwined. He smiled at the memory, knowing he'd think of it much in the many years to come. A surge of emotion settled inside his chest. He didn't feel so sure about Aisla anymore. Isobel was the one running in his mind.

Isobel was having an inner debate herself. She was deciding on whether to finally admit her feelings. She knew that she had been saying that for quite some time, always changing her mind at the last moment. She did not want to do that anymore and was figuring out the best way to go about it. Dissuading him from his decision about Aisla hadn't worked out, so that wasn't an option. She could try to show him how much they differed from each other.

"Alpin?" Isobel asked. He was riding the horse slower than he had the entire journey, it was almost as if the horse was dragging itself forward.

"Aye?" Alpin asked, lost in his own dilemma.

"Remember yer love for painting?" Isobel asked.

"Aye, of course. Da didn't approve so I quit." He said, remembering the argument his father and he had had over it.

"It's really hard to find people with a passion for painting. Some even hate it, ye know." Isobel mused.

"Aye, it is quite difficult." Alpin said. "Which reminds me, Aisla paints too, ye know?"

"Oh, that's wonderful." Isobel said, discouraged.

They crossed a few more fields and Isobel tried her plan again.

"Does she like dogs?" Isobel asked, knowing Alpin detested them.

"Nay, thank heaven for that." He said absent-mindedly. She was surprised that a conversation about Aisla wasn't interesting him as much as it usually did.

"Thank heaven indeed." Isobel said and her shoulders slumped in surrender. Perhaps Aisla was his perfect match. Isobel hated painting and absolutely adored dogs.

They rode a while longer. Alpin was trying to put off the inevitable and he knew it. Although he had said he loved Aisla, somehow his mind was trying to communicate that it wasn't true. He was growing doubtful about his decision. He was riding slower than he should be. What had gotten into him? A day ago, if Alpin had been so close to Campbell, he would've raced his horse to ask for Aisla's hand in marriage. A day ago, however, he had not seen Isobel in a new light.

Isobel herself was trying to solve the puzzle of whether to try another tactic or outright declare her love. Her head was resting against Alpin's back and his scent was heady. She inhaled it deeply, loving it. She steadied herself and decided honesty was the best way forward for her and them.

"Alpin?" She said, for once not willing to back down or even allow herself to consider it.

"Aye?" He said, his tone flat and empty.

Isobel noticed how he wasn't as excited as he should be, considering he was about to make the biggest decision of his life. Perhaps this was a good sign, and she was encouraged even further.

"We've been friends for a while now, right?" Isobel said. "We've known each other for long."

"We're here." Alpin said, resigned, looking at the houses in front of him.

"Aye, now we're here. Together, as friends like we've always been." Isobel said, not understanding what he meant.

"Nay, Isobel." He said, a bit irritated. His inner conflict was baffling him and aggravating him. "We're here. We're at Campbell."

Isobel stopped rambling, realising finally what he said. She was too late and she knew it. Alpin was perplexed, Isobel was heartbroken. Together they entered Campbell, the journey ending. Alpin was not ready for what was to come. He did not want to be here anymore. The prospect of Aisla as his bride was not making him feel warm as he thought it would. He turned to look at

Isobel, her face looked forlorn and lost, and here he found the warmth he was missing. Aisla had never evoked that within him.

***

They reached the outside of the Laird's estate after taking directions from a shepherd in the outskirts. Isobel had lost all hope and now looked forward, resigned and willing herself not to break down. She would be strong. Her best friend since she was a baby was taking a step forward into his future. She would not tarnish it with tears and unnecessary revelations of how she felt. She smiled softly, remembering how, after such a long struggle she had finally been so close to telling Alpin how she felt. Yet, of course fate was cruel, and that was the moment they reached Campbell. It was a sign she could not ignore. They were not meant to be.

Alpin wondered why he was even going to meet the Laird of Campbell when his heart was feeling as unsettled as it did. Could he turn around now? Run away and hide, not face these responsibilities. They were outside the estate and the guard ushered their horse forward to the main door. They got off and headed inside. They were in the main corridor. Huge paintings hung on both sides of the stone wall, a lavish carpet of burgundy colour lay on the floor. A maid led them into the Great Hall, where a cosy fire burned, basking its surrounding with warmth. Isobel and Alpin were famished and tired. A maid brought them a tray with hot tea and almond cake. They sat and ate, the cake melting in their mouths.

After they had finished eating, they sat waiting for the Laird. No one came to inform them of his whereabouts, and Isobel suspected that no one had informed him of their arrival. Isobel got off the chair and went towards the fire to warm her hands. A few seconds passed and a voice reached them from outside the hall.

"I ASKED YE TO LOCATE HER AT ALL COSTS!" A man was screaming, at a servant no doubt.

A second passed before they screamed again,

"DO YE HAVE ANY IDEA HOW HUMILIATING IT WILL BE WHEN PEOPLE FIND OUT THE DAUGHTER OF A LAIRD RAN AWAY??" The voice roared. Isobel and Alpin rushed from the Great Hall upon hearing this.

Chapter 11

Isobel wondered what was going on. They came into the hallway and saw that a man, no doubt the Laird, had hoisted a man up off his feet by the front of his shirt. He was jerking the man back and forth, screaming,

"FIND HER! FIND HER!"

The Laird dropped the man on the floor and turned around. He snarled when he saw two strangers staring at him in shock. Isobel ran to help the man off the floor. The Laird eyed her with disgust and Isobel stared back, bestowing the same upon him.

"Who are ye? Who let ye in?" The Laird barked at them.

"I am Alpin McGregor, son of Angus, The Laird of McGregor." Alpin introduced himself, "This is my friend, Isobel."

"I am The Laird of Campbell, at yer service." The Laird said, his voice less harsh after finding out the importance of Alpin's status. The McGregor's were a strong clan, financially and otherwise.

"We're actually here about, Aisla, Sir." Alpin said unsurely.

"Do ye know where she is?! Has she contacted ye??" The Laird asked, his eyes crazy.

"Aye, she was staying with us for a while, as ye know." Alpin said, confused about what was happening.

"Stay? I knew? Well, I had no idea she was there! Had I, I would've come to get her!" The Laird said madly.

Isobel was starting to understand what was going on here. Her father had not known she was there. She had run away. Her suspicions were confirmed when the Laird answered Alpin's next query.

"Sir, were ye not the one to have her visit us? For a future union between our clans? Through our marriage?" Alpin asked, feeling stupider by the minute. He was taking a while to get to speed with the situation. He felt even more foolish when the Laird burst out laughing. He could hear Isobel laughing softly behind him, but stopped when he glared at her.

"AH LADDIE! She conned ye into giving her lodging! My daughter ran away three weeks ago!! I don't know what union she talked about but it ain't supported by me!" The laird guffawed. Isobel feared he was becoming hysterical.

"Wait, ye mean to say Aisla was not hunting? She was running away?" Alpin asked, still not believing it.

"Quite slow for a future laird, ye are lad. I am saying my daughter, Aisla ran away." The laird said, emphasising each word. "She's already on a boat half across the country, I bet!"

Isobel could swear she saw tears glistening in the laird's eyes. He was bordering on breaking down, but was laughing to hold himself together.

"That is- "Alpin started before the laird slapped him on his shoulder.

"Mighty bullocks! Isn't it?" He choked out through another fit of laughter.

Alpin was enraged. She had never seen him so angry. Before he could express his rage, a coachman entered the hallway.

"Sire, The Sutherlands are here. And the shepherd had sent word a party of warriors are not so far behind, they're from McGregor, I believe." He said and left.

Isobel felt her heart free fall into anxiety and saw the same expression pass across

Alpin's face, fleetingly, before he composed himself.

"Splendid! It's a party now!!" The Laird boosted, heading towards the door to greet the unexpected guests.

Alpin would not have worried about the Sutherlands, since there would be no marriage with the Campbells. He felt betrayed that Aisla had lied to him and deceived him. But he also felt a sense of ease. He no longer had to marry her. His ease increased when he looked at Isobel. She was frowning and he knew why. His father would never bring warriors with him, unless something outrageous had happened. Alpin and Isobel only hoped it wasn't unsalvageable.

***

The Sutherlands had found no reason to argue with The Campbells or complain about Alpin's involvement with another girl. The Campbell girl had run away and no marriage could happen. They had been led to The Great Hall to feast until The Laird of Campbell would welcome the McGregors, and understand why they had brought warriors along.

Isobel and Alpin stood to the side, on the stairs at the entrance. The wind was chilly as it would soon be dark. The Laird of Campbell paced around the porch, waiting for Alpin's father to arrive. He was stressed about his daughter. He was aggravated and did not want to be here. He wanted to be outside searching for her. The two had always been somewhat estranged; he did not know the extent of it was this high. He saw horses approaching. The McGregors had come.

Alpin and Isobel went down to meet his father and find out what catastrophe had occurred. The horses stopped in front of them and Agnus McGregor dismounted swiftly. The warriors followed his lead and flanked him, three on each side. The others remained on their horses, waiting for any sign of distress to leap into action. It was an entire battalion. Agnus looked raving mad as he came towards his son. Alpin feared that his father had come following Alpin's misbehaviour with The Sutherlands, who were not seated inside, waiting to complain about him.

"Where is the girl?" Angus barked, his anger evident.

The Laird of Campbell rushed to his side, quite evidently feeling inferior. The McGregors were a mighty clan with great influence and power.

"My Aisla? Have ye seen her?" Laird Campbell asked, hysterical yet again.

"Seen her? I quite obviously have! Wretched girl, she stole from McGregor!!" Angus roared.

Alpin and Isobel looked at each other with confusion, not knowing what Angus meant.

"Steal? My girl would do no such thing, Sir." Laird Campbell said, unconvincingly. He had his doubt, knowing she had left with little to no riches.

"Our lady's wedding tiara! It is missing and Aisla is the only person who can be answerable, as none of our own would ever do such a thing! No one dares step inside the forbidden premises!" Angus screamed, unable to lower his voice.

"Sir, if ye could just follow me inside." Laird Campbell suggested, eyeing the warriors with fear. "It will allow us to discuss this in a civilized manner, privately."

Angus signalled two of his men to follow him while the rest remained on their guard outside. Isobel nudged Alpin forward, for he stood frozen in shock. Aisla had stolen from them? Whatever Isobel had reported about her was true. He was disgusted with Aisla and himself for not believing Isobel over her. He moved forward, taking Isobel's hand in his, for support, and for comfort against the emotions he did not understand.

Isobel rushed inside, led by Alpin as they followed Laird Campbell's direction. She was relieved that her suspicions were confirmed but was also concerned. This would lead to matters getting worse. Alpin was definitely not marrying Aisla, and his chances with The Sutherlands were diminished too. She would have time before another girl came knocking on the McGregor's door. The only problem that remained was the stolen tiara. Laird Campbell led them towards the Great Hall and she wondered if that was the smartest idea, considering the Sutherlands were also in there.

The Sutherlands rose when they entered, and Angus halted mid-step, retreating.

"Laird Sutherland, how surprising to find ye here." Angus said, his embarrassment quite evident.

"Laird McGregor, since ye did not think to bestow upon us the courtesy of your union with the Campbells, I decided I should come give my congratulations in person. Seeing as it is them ye choose over us." He said, snidely. His displeasure with the McGregors, son and father, was visible.

"I apologise for not letting ye know beforehand, however, no such union will be taking place." Angus clarified, eyeing Laird Campbell vehemently, who cowered under his gaze.

"Is that so?" Laird Sutherland asked, his anger lessoned.

Isobel groaned internally. She had not realized the Sutherlands would still be interested, even after the incident that had taken place on their campsite.

"Aye, Campbell's girl stole from us." Angus said, scowling.

"Sir, may I remind ye, ye have no substantial proof to support your accusations against my daughter!" Laird Campbell snapped. He was feeling humiliated.

"She was seen in the forbidden corridors." Alpin said. He had remained silent throughout the conversation, until now.

"Isobel saw her, did ye not?" He turned to Isobel.

"Aye." Isobel said, her voice soft.

"Go on, Isobel. Tell them." Angus said, trusting her to be truthful.

"I was cleaning the corridors and the room present within the forbidden premises when I saw Aisla lurking there. She left in a hurry upon seeing me." Isobel said, remembering the event as well as if it were yesterday.

"I will not listen to a maid accusing my daughter. We cannot take her word for it!" Laird Campbell said indignantly.

"Ah sir, I pay ye to be respectful. After all they hold this maid in high esteem, these McGregors, seeing as she dilly dallies with their only son, deep in the woods." Laird Sutherland said mockingly. Clearly, he still believed Isobel and Alpin were having a torrid affair, away from the public eye.

Isobel rolled her eyes, wishing that were true. She couldn't help feeling ashamed, though, that these strange men accused her of immoral conduct. Alpin became angry at this. Before he could sound his protest, his father did.

"Sir, I ask ye to be a bit more respectful towards our kin. Isobel is a friend of the family, near and dear to us. I demand ye treat her with the same conduct ye do us. I do not suggest ye think they were involved in foul play. My son and Isobel would never leave the house or run away to have a relationship." Angus said, his voice venomous.

Isobel felt grateful that the Laird himself was vouching for her in front of people far more important than her.

"Yer right, they don't run away! It's the Campbell's daughter that does!" Laird Sutherland boomed out in laughter and his men followed.

"Run away?" Angus asked, looking at his son.

"Aye, she had not been sent by her father for the purpose we thought. That was a ploy to make us give her lodging. Her father was completely unaware of it." Alpin informed his father, whose face became ghastly with shock. Alpin only felt more foolish, announcing it out loud.

"Aye, aye! But I assure ye, when Aisla is back, she will be more than honoured to marry into and serve an influential clan such as yers, Laird McGregor." Laird Campbell said, his eyes looking at Alpin with greed. Isobel knew he was no doubt seeing the centuries of power and riches the McGregor's held.

"Yer daughter? Laddie, discuss her marriage when ye locate her!" Laird Sutherland said through chuckles. "Laird McGregor, now that all confusion is cleared, I think ye and I both know it's best for our clans to come together." Laird Sutherland said, his eyes greedier than Campbell's.

Alpin felt naked under their lustful gaze, horrified at the prospect of marrying into such families. He'd never even met Laird Sutherland's daughter. How could he be finalising the marriage without having them meet? Did she not get a say?

"Laird Sutherland, I think it's best if we talk about this later." Angus said, seeing their true intentions.

"Sir, I assure ye, together with yer warriors and mine, we'll find Aisla in no time." Laird Campbell butted in.

"Ah Campbell, yer being sleazy. McGregor's have no respect for such men neither do the Sutherlands, a perfect match. My beautiful, young daughter is the best suitor far and wide." Laird Sutherland boasted.

"Sir, we have never even met her." Alpin said, his annoyance evident. "I hardly think she'll encourage this without having given her consent."

"Oh nay! My daughter is obedient and too young to know better for herself than her da." Laird Sutherland assured him.

"How young?" Alpin asked, feeling perplexed at an idea of such an obedient child.

"Why, she is fourteen this winter. Perfect age for a bride!" Laird Sutherland boasted, looking at Campbell.

Isobel stared at him with pure shock. As did Alpin and Angus.

"She is a child!" Angus said, horrified.

"Ye will have no complaint." Laird Sutherland said avertedly.

"With Aisla. Ye will have no complain with Aisla." Laird Campbell added.

"If she's ever found!' Sutherland laughed again.

"She will be! She's not a child, unlike yer daughter." Campbell snapped back.

"Men, calm yerself." Angus said, unheard through their bickering.

"She's almost of age."

"In a millennium ye mean!"

"At least she is happy with her family!"

"Take that back, ye imbecile!"

"ENOUGH!!" Alpin roared, silencing everyone.

Everyone stared at him with shock, afraid to say more. Angus looked relieved to have the men quieted down.

"We are done here! Da, we need not meddle in such business for the sake of a tiara. We'll be leaving now." Alpin said, looking at everyone. Angus stood.

"That does it, laddies! Thank ye for yer time." Angus bowed, sarcastically. He turned on his heels and walked out with the guards following him.

Alpin nudged Isobel and took hold of her hand again. He couldn't understand why but he wanted to be in contact with her, touching her in any way possible. They went after his father and everyone mounted their horses for departure.

"Maddening bunch, isn't it?" Angus said, appalled. "Come on, Alpin let's go home. Isobel, ye can ride with me."

"She'll ride with me, Da." Alpin said, getting on his own horse.

"Alright. Although, girl ye nearly gave yer da a heart attack. Why on earth did ye come after Alpin?" Angus asked and Isobel blushed, her secret out.

"I apologise." Isobel said, hiding her embarrassment. Angus raced his horse towards the outskirts, his warriors following him.

Alpin stared at her intently, waiting for her to come forth about her lie. She did not make any move to do so and Alpin asked, "Da, didn't send ye?" Alpin moved a step towards her.

"Nay, he didn't." Isobel said, not meeting his eyes.

"He did not ask ye to accompany me?" Alpin asked taking another two steps towards her.

"Nay, he didn't." Isobel said, still not facing him.

"Ye came on yer own decision?" Alpin asked, again taking a step to her.

"Nay." Isobel said, her heart racing. Would he be upset with her?

"Why did ye come, Isobel?" Alpin asked, standing in front of her. His voice was silky and Isobel's resolve wavered. She wanted to tell him, right then that she loved him.

"I don't know." She said, cowardly.

"Look at me." Alpin said, lifting her face with his index finger. He gave her a smouldering look and asked again, "Why did ye come?"

Isobel could not hold back. It would be injustice to lie to such a handsome face any longer. His gaze made her insides curl and she decided to reveal her love at last.

"Because I love ye. Because I am in love with ye." Isobel said, a burden lifted off her chest. She was prepared for the rejection.

Alpin inhaled sharply and crushed her mouth with his. He kissed her softly, not rushing. Isobel reciprocated, overcoming the sudden surprise and unexpected response. She curled her hands into his hair, and opened her mouth for him. He wrapped his arms around her waist, crushing her to him. Alpin did not want to let go. He had realised why he couldn't envision a life without her. Unbeknownst to him, he too had fallen in love with her. When, he did not know. How, he couldn't tell. He only knew he loved her too much to live without her. They pulled apart, gasping for breath and Isobel rested her head on his chest, where he cradled her.

Isobel wondered if he felt the same. The kiss had been her first and the most magical moment in her life. The wait had been worth it after all. She was glad she had revealed her heart to him, no matter how he felt.

"I love ye too, Isobel. I don't know why it took me so long to understand my own heart, when it was right there in front of me in your hands." Alpin said, revelling in the warmth of her embrace.

Isobel gushed, hearing that his love for her was as true as hers for him. She pulled away, looking into his eyes, her smile matching his. He caressed her face and placed his hand on her neck, kissing her again. Deeply and persuasively this time. Isobel lost her train of thought and kissed him back greedily, making up for lost time.

A cough interrupted their kiss and they pulled apart, feeling shy.

"Came back to see what the holdup was!" Angus boasted, the warriors snickering behind him.

Alpin and Isobel got on his horse silently, avoiding Angus' eyes. He grinned, meaning he approved without objection. He had never seen Isobel as his daughter in law, having always seen her as a daughter but she was the best match for his son. The battalion, Alpin and Angus readied to depart.

"Seems like we won't be needing a suitor after all!" Angus laughed out loud, as they raced through the winds back to McGregor.

Alpin's laugh matched his father's as Isobel buried her head in his shoulders. Together, they made way back to their home, their journey finally ending. Alpin mused over why it took him so long to realise what he felt. He recalled all his memories, Isobel present in each as the lead role. When he had fallen in love with his best friend, he could not decipher. This trip had never been about Aisla, it had been about finding his way to Isobel. His friend, his love and his family. She was the one he'd marry. Alpin laughed out loud and Isobel giggled, basking in his euphoria. He raced his horse next his father's. His father passed him a wink, as they made their hasty way towards McGregor, to home.

Early Bird Notification List

Thank you for reading Highland Dreams. To join my early bird notification list of all my new releases, please click on the links below:

http://www.jamiemacseaver.com

Please like my Facebook fan page:

https://www.facebook.com/jamiemacseaver

Please follow me on Twitter:

https://www.twitter.com/jamiemacseaver

Please follow me on Amazon Author Central:

http://amazon.com/author/jamiemacseaver
Books By Jamie MacSeaver

Highland Dreams

Click the links below to download on Amazon:

Amazon.com

Amazon.co.uk

Highland Rendezvous

Click the links below to download on Amazon:

Amazon.com

Amazon.co.uk

Highland Identity

Click the links below to download on Amazon:

Amazon.com

Amazon.co.uk

Highland Rendezvous Preview

The Damsel Unstressed

"Curse ye, Bryn ye darn numpty!" Bryn Menzies groaned, trying to figure out which way to go. She had left her lands, wanting to go for an evening horse ride and now she was conveniently lost. It was getting darker by the minute, the moonlight the only glow for her to see from. Bryn knew for sure this was going to get only harder and harder. She could already imagine the worried and angry look on her dear father's face as he wondered where she was and searched for her.

She knew there was no hope for her to get back to her clan in the darkness that was slowly engulfing her. She regretted coming into the forest without a lantern or a guard. Bryn was the only and cherished daughter of The Laird of Menzies, Angus. She was spoilt rotten but had grown up to be like her father, mannered, just, and fearsome and a leader. Having grown up with a warrior upbringing, Bryn was more than capable of handling a night out alone in the forest, something she was prone to indulging in now and then, sneakily. However, she was not keen on the idea of the castle being in a frenzy as they searched for her. Her father would no doubt send out his men to locate her and ensure she was safe.

Knowing there was no other choice, she stopped her horse in a clearing, with the sound of the lake reaching her ears like a soft hum, and tied it to a tree bark. She scanned the area, squinting her eyes to see clearly and found the perfect branches to break off and start a fire. She gathered the twigs and wood she broke off and threw it in a pile on the floor. She found two stones on the soft ground and rubbed them together to spark a fire. With how the night was progressing, Bryn knew the wind would become chilly and make her feel cold. The fire crackled, leaving its surrounding environment aflame with light. Bryn enjoyed starting fires, the warmth they provided was one Bryn was a fan of. Every now and then, Bryn would head out into the woods to spend a night. Yet, she always took her father's permission and never went without his consent and knowledge. Bryn took off her plaid and lay it on the ground to lie down on. She placed her dagger and sword next to her head in case an unwelcome visitor came by at night. She wouldn't be surprised if there were nomads wandering these very woods, this part of the land was infamous for its lurking visitors, always ready to strike for riches and bounty.

Tonight had been about Bryn getting away from the estate that only spoke of the battles the Menzies were raging against the Lamont clan, in the east. A subject Bryn was not keen on being indulged in. She knew that her father was compassionate, yet, driven by the need to protect his own clan he would always attack other clans. If it were up to Bryn she would abolish the notion of battles and urge everyone to live together in harmony and union. She hadn't planned on riding out so far, but a snake had scared her horse into a frenzy leading them into a dense part of the forest, with no idea of where to head from there on. Bryn was a fierce girl, who feared no one but the wrath of doing ill to others. Yet, she knew how scary it would be if she was lying on enemy land, and someone came and found her. She was twenty one years of age with black hair that hung till her waist in thick locks with hazel eyes.

Bryn was not scared of a man coming and attacking her, if anything she feared for his life in face of her knife skill. But she knew her father would never let her hear the end of riding into enemy land, unprotected and on her own. She hoped this night would pass without any incidents and she could sneak into her chamber early in the morning without anyone except the night guard noticing, whom she could easily bribe with a double portion at dinner.

Bryn looked at the sky, her arms folded underneath her head, and admired the sky full of stars. The silence was one that she welcomed whole heartedly, being used to the loud and gruff voices of her household that was always hosting people of the clan for celebrations, discussions and anything really.

Some time passed and Bryn felt her eyes shutting close when the sound of leaves rustling shook her awake. She got up with a start, picking her sword up as she went and looked around for an intruder or worse a wild animal.

She waited for a minute and saw a shadow moving in the woods.

"Who are ye? Show yerself!" Bryn said, her voice confident showing no fear.

A man, with a large body, came forth from the dark woods. The light from the fire showed Bryn a glimpse of his face and she asked, "Who are ye?!" She pointed her sword in his direction, ready to strike. She saw he had blonde hair with hints of brown streaks in it. His eyes were green, twinkling in the glow of the flame.

"I am Niall, who are ye?" The man asked, his voice deep and sombre.

"I am Bryn. What do ye seek?" Bryn asked, not letting down her guard. She saw no danger for he had not withdrawn his own sword that hung by his side in its belt.

"I can ask ye the same girl." Niall said, his voice showing a hint of irony. Bryn noticed he was being hesitant to answer her queries. She noticed he traveled alone, as no one had followed him into the clearing. Would he have attacked her if she hadn't heard his steps?

"Are ye alone? Speak the truth." Bryn said, straightening her shoulders to show she was not petite and could over power him. She hoped it wouldn't come to that, knowing it would be a difficult task.

"As alone as one can hope to be. Are ye?" Niall asked, his eyes scanning the area and following on the plaid that lay on the ground, although he could not see the colors properly.

"Aye, I be alone." Bryn said, "But I am armed."

"Put yer sword away, I mean ye no harm. I am lone and I wish to only warm myself in the fire ye have started." Niall said, eyeing Bryn's face and looking into her eyes to show his sincerity to not harm her.

"If that be the case then go ahead, Niall." Bryn offered, putting down her sword but still holding on to it. She picked up her plaid off the ground and folded it. She knew she just might be in the Lamont territory and Niall seeing her plaid colors would bring no good.

"Where do ye come from?" Bryn asked, wanting to be sure about who she was dealing with.

"Not far, my clan is just around the edge of the forest." Niall said, conveniently not giving a name. The Lamont's also resided within this territory and Bryn was not taking any chances.

"What clan?" Bryn asked.

"None that you've ever heard about, we're a small settlement of independents residing together." Niall said, without hesitation. "Ye?"

Bryn halted before answering, deciding concealing her true identity was the best choice in this situation. If there was anything Bryn had learned it was too always play out all your cards smartly.

"Duggal clan." Bryn said, remembering about the prestigious clan in the west that lived far away from them.

"Then what are ye doing out here, alone?" Niall asked, looking into the fire with an intent scrutiny.

"I was riding and me horse got scared by a snake and lost its way." Bryn explained, feeling foolish for not keeping a better grip onto the horse. It would've saved her from this night alone in the woods with a complete stranger, who was not making any move to leave.

"Ah, a rider are we?" Niall said, looking away from the fire and towards her. Bryn noticed how the fire made the brown in his hair look more evident and striking against his pale complexion. He was quite handsome, that she had to admit.

"Aye." Bryn said, smugly. Riding was one of her many talents. She was royalty and of course she impressed peasants like Niall.

They became silent for a little while till Bryn cleared her throat. She had given him more than enough time to warm up.

"What are ye doing out here?" Bryn asked, making conversation so she could ask him to leave without being rude.

"I was out hunting. This place be crawling with mountain lion and bears, feisty ones." Niall said, his eyes looking into the dark woods almost as if he could see the animal waiting to pounce.

A chill ran down Bryn's spine when she heard this, having a fear of wild animals. Hunting had always been her weak point having once been attacked by a mountain lion as a child. Her father had killed it off and had the skin made into a coat for Bryn but alongside it she still had a scar on her half body from the attack. From that day forth she had sworn to never go hunting again. If

Bryn had known she'd end up lost in a part of the forest with lions and bears, she would've chosen to happily stay in the castle and listen to the boring and dull political discussions her father loved to have.

"Are these lands populated by these beasts?" Bryn asked, gulping.

"Aye, a whole lot of them." Niall said, smiling slightly at her evident fear. The smile shook Bryn out of her anxious state and she sat up straighter, showing she did not fear anything.

"Best be to stick together till morning. It would be a shame if ye run into an animal out there in the dark." Bryn said, trying to show she was doing him a favor when she clearly wanted him to stay to protect her.

"Ye are too kind." Niall said and bowed his head lightly towards her.

A Truce

The sun rose from the Highland Mountains, shining its rays upon the clearing in which Bryn slept, her sword held tightly to her chest, ready to strike any animal or human who dare attack her. When the light became too much for her to continue sleeping, Bryn woke up and saw the fire had died out already some time during the night. She yawned, rubbing her eyes to shake away the remaining sleepiness. Her back throbbed from lying still on the hard forest floor. Bryn missed her plush and soft bed back at her father's estate.

She turned to see her horse was missing and got up, furious that Niall had dared to steal it and run away. She would make him pay enough so that he regretted the day he had decided to con her and steal from her. She threw her plaid into the woods, not wanting to be dragged down by carrying it and searched around for any sight of her horse. Her sword was ready to attack Niall the moment she saw him. Much to her embarrassment, Niall stood not far from the clearing, near the lake. He watched over her horse as it drank water from the lake and Bryn turned red in humiliation knowing Bryn no doubt knew why she had gotten up so quickly.

"Top o' the morning to you, Lady Bryn." Niall said, his eyes glinting with humor. Bryn held her head high as she walked towards him, ignoring any hint he implied towards her over reaction.

"Morning." Bryn said, coolly. "What are ye nibbling on?"

Bryn felt famished, she hadn't eaten since lunch yesterday with her father. She wondered why her father hadn't come searching for her yet.

"Would ye like some?" Niall offered her some loganberries he had plucked and Bryn took them, her stomach rumbling with hunger pangs.

"It's light enough for ye to be safe in the woods, out hunting." Bryn said, looking steadily away from him. "We'll be leaving then. Thank ye for the company."

She made to take her horse's leash in her hand and Niall stopped her. He rested his hand on hers lightly but Bryn took offence.

"Brace yerself, laddie. I have an arm as strong as one of the finest men in all of Scotland." Bryn said, the warning clear in her eyes. "Ye won't know what hit ye."

"I have no intent to stop ye just that if ye even know where the road is." Niall said, folding his arms smugly. "If ye do, be my guest and leave."

Bryn was about to retort with a smart comment but deliberated when she realized that she in fact did not know where the road was. Bryn groaned internally and regretted coming this far into the forest. It would've been better for here to have stayed there instead of wandering out alone. It would've also made it easier for her father to find her that way. Bryn wondered how wise would it be to go on her own and find her way she went. She was not good with directions, but she was capable of navigating by her memory. Niall noticed her inner conflict of putting aside her ego and asking for help or heading out blind into unknown territory. He decided to offer help instead of making her ask for it.

"I have to head out on the trail me self. Can ye offer me a ride in return for directions?" Niall asked, making sure to sound humble. "I don't have anything else to offer to ye."

He had noticed Bryn was a ferocious woman with a strong confidence that he dare not challenge. Niall admired her courage and stubbornness but wouldn't admit to her, ever.

"Aye, I can give ye a ride." Brynn said. "Ye can thank me later."

They got on the horse, Bryn riding it and headed into the direction Niall pointed out. A slight problem halted their ride. Bryn had no idea where she was, the road unfamiliar with both sides leading to places Bryn did not know. How would she be able to find her way home, unaware as she felt?

***

"I assure ye this is the right way!" Bryn snapped, pointing in the opposite direction that Niall was telling her to ride towards. "Ye need to listen to me!"

"I assure ye that this is the right one!" Niall snapped back, feeling slightly irritated with Bryn. He all but decided to leave her out here on her own when a small commotion in the woods stopped their arguments, voices that came right towards them in the form of a band of thieves hoisting their arrows and swords. Niall turned around, his eyes raging angry as he saw the thieves headed towards them. He swung himself on Bryn's horse and helped her up before setting off to out run the thieves that tried to pursue them. Niall directed the horse back towards the wood, as Bryn held on to his waist tightly to avoid falling. She was cringing inside at her foolishness to have left home at all, for now she was trying to avoid bandits to save her life. Niall led their horse into the forest, the dense woods providing them with enough cover to hide out and protect themselves.

When no one was heard except for them, they got off the horse and scanned the area around them to see if anyone was following them. They were deeper inside the woods than they had been last night. Niall had a look of concentration on his face as he took Bryn's dagger from her belt.

"I'll gie ye a skelpit lug!" Bryn snapped, outraged that he took her dagger without permission.

"Keep the heid!" Niall snapped back, "Ready yer sword for any visitor that might come, unannounced."

Bryn glared at him, feeling insulted and angry but continued to do as he told. She took out her sword, hoisting it in her hand to be prepared to strike. She gave the woods around them a quick look, her eyes looking for any strange presence that could endanger their lives.

"I think they're gone…" Bryn said, keeping her voice low.

"Aye, I think so too." Niall said loudly and put her dagger inside his own belt.

"That's mine, I'll be taking it back now, thank ye very much." Bryn said, holding out her hand for him to give back her dagger.

"Ye ca have it if ye so desire, best be able to defend yerself alone I suppose if another band of thieves comes." Niall said, holding out her dagger. He knew how easy it would be for thieves to capture her, if she were to be on her own.

Bryn buckled, realizing she could not protect herself, on her own, from too many bandits. Niall, again, noticed her inner debate on whether to let down her ego and guard or to go on her own, without him and protection. Niall knew she was his responsibility now and he couldn't let her fending for herself, without any help. Besides Niall couldn't deny that despite of her annoying attitude, he respected her valor and wanted to ensure she reached her home safely. He shuddered to think what would happen to her if another band of thieves found her and this time did capture her.

"I'll take ye back to yer home, I know the way as well as anyone who lives here. We'll have to find our way back to the road." Niall said, smiling encouragingly to show he meant well.

"I suppose." Bryn said, and smiled back at him. "Let's do it then. Shall we?"

Bryn felt her heart soften towards her companion, Niall. He did not have to do this, but he was choosing to, despite Bryn being less than welcome. She respected those who thought of other's safety and well-being alongside theirs. He did not have to accompany her on her way home, but he had decided to, knowing the dangerous bandits and nomads that crawled the highlands. They got up on her horse and set off, in search for the road that would lead Bryn back to her home and her life that awaited. Bryn was grateful, that on this lonely and tiresome journey, she had Niall to turn to for companionship and comradery.

They smiled at each other, an unspoken understanding blossoming between them.

The story continues…

Amazon.com

Amazon.co.uk

Highland Identity Preview

Meeting the Laird

Mahri was so exhausted she walked slowly. Not for the first time, she couldn't find a place to sleep last night. The barn she was using had a sick calf, and a healer occupied it well past daylight.

She spent the night on the floor of the forest edge under one of the bushes that still had leaves. But it was getting colder every night. Soon, now that winter was coming, she would have to walk to the next village and look for work in a cottage. Somewhere there was room for her through the winter months.

Mahri knew how her life changed with the season. On her own since the age of twelve, when warriors scoured the countryside and killed her parents, she had learned to fend for herself.

And fend for herself she had. She worked when she could and stole when she couldn't.

She could defend herself against most men and had excellent lungs for screaming when she couldn't. No job was beneath her. She gladly cleaned out horse stalls and pigsties for a place to sleep and food to eat.

She was not naïve. Experience had hardened her against relying on others. It always ended in disappointment or danger. If she lived and survived on her own, she needn't worry about others doing their part.

Mahri pushed the thought from her mind when she smelled a loaf of bread. It was heavenly. As if on cue, her stomach Rumbled and her mouth watered. It called to her and she was powerless to stop her feet from following the smell.

On the way, she passed an alley. She heard one tiny voice crying and another tiny voice shushing. Mahri looked up at the cottage, bread cooling on the sill of a window then she looked down alley where she heard the anguished voices of children.

There was no real decision to make, although her empty stomach would disagree. She walked toward the voices slowly. She didn't want to scare them but she also couldn't see in the dark of the new moon. Her progress was hampered by the dirt of the alley marked with deep puddles of water and large rocks. She put her hand on the wall while she tested each step before taking it.

"Hello," Mahri said in the gentlest voice she could muster. "Dinnae be afraid. Ah came tae help."

The alley went quiet as the two children must have become mute with fear. Her hand kept feeling her way down one side of the alley. She talked to them so they wouldn't jump when she got close them.

"Aam coming tae ye. Dinnae be afraid. Ah just want tae make sure ye are all right, an' then Ah will leave." Mahri had no intention of leaving. She just knew they were scared enough without her adding another layer to the fear.

Mahri felt the alley end and began searching with her foot for the children's location. Her eyes slowly adjusted enough for her to see them in the other corner from her.

She sat on her haunches. There were two boys, twins, clinging to each other, eyes looking at her in fear. She had seen eyes like that many times before. Eyes that looked too large for their small, undernourished faces.

The boys each had on a shirt, torn and dirty and a few sizes too large. Their pants were another problem. One had more holes in his pants than the other but neither one had enough fabric covering their legs to call them pants. They had nothing on their feet.

"Ah am Mahri. Dae ye ken yer names and how auld ye are?"

Both boys shook their head, no. Mahri reached out to check the boys for fever. They both jumped. She berated herself for putting her hands on them without explaining herself first. They weren't warm enough.

Mahri took off her cloak and wanted to laugh. Or maybe cry. The thing had holes in it and tears along the bottom and at the seams. It was so worn; its next job should have been in a barn to keep animals warm.

She tucked it over the boys' bodies and around their backs. "Leave it where it is. It will keep yer body warm wrapped aroond you. Aam gonnae tae get ye something tae eat. Ah willnae be gone long."

Mahri stood and picked her way out of the alley back to the street. It must have been late – there was only silence. Not a soul was on the street or outside a cottage. She was alone. Mahri looked up at the sky. With no moon, she had to walk carefully even after she emerged from the alley. She picked her way to the cottage where the boys' hunger would be satisfied bread. She tried to walk by with a practiced nonchalant step, grabbed the bread and walked on. Once she cleared the cottage, she ran as best she could in the darkness. This time, she made it down the alley much faster.

The boys could smell the bread before she reached them. She heard them stir and sniff. She crouched in front of them and tore the bread in half, one half for each boy. Their arms came out to take the bread. Mahri smiled, then sighed.

She heard a noise behind her and shot up, standing in front of the boys to shield them. . Mahri would protect the boys and their food from any vagrants set on stealing from them.

She felt a large hand grab the fabric of her dress at her shoulder, gripping both with force. She bent her knees and raised her fists. This wasn't Mahri's first street fight.

Mahri stomped on the vagrant's toes and elbowed him in the stomach, trying in vain to cause him to loosen his grip. She pulled back her elbow and landed a good punch in his stomach, but still he wouldn't loosen his grip. This was no scrawny vagrant. His body was hard. Her punch made no dent in his stomach, but her knuckles felt as if they were broken.

Mahri's attention was drawn to the boys in the corner of the alley. They were crying. She hoped they ate their bread before their fear took over. Somehow, she thought they didn't.

When she drew her attention back to her attacker, she was defeated. She looked up at him. Something shiny caught her eye. The light was so dim she was sure she was seeing things.

He had the unmistakable dress of a Laird. He wore a pin that was a cur out of a wolf. Mahri muttered to herself. She was staring before the Laird of clan Stewart. She took a deep breath and waited.

His hand had moved to her upper arm and he gripped her with force. She vowed she wouldn't wince. That might encourage him to hold tighter.

"Explain yerself," came the deep strong voice of her captor.

Mahri had never backed down from a fight and she was not going to begin now. Didn't this man have more important things to do than go after a woman and two children? Like sleep? "Ah might ask ye th' same question. Why might th' Laird be in a dark alley sae late at night?"

He laughed. A deep, rich sound that made everyone around him want to do the same. But they didn't. Mahri thought they probably didn't dare.

"Did ye just ask yer Laird tae explain himself?" Oh, she hated when men use that tone with her. Yes, she was homeless and dirty and she just stole bread, but couldn't he use a civil tone?

She wasn't a murderer.

"Ah did."

Liam's face became serious. He pulled Mahri aside so he could get a look at the boys behind her.

"Are they yer bairnes?"

"Nae."

"'En how are you acquainted?"

"We arnae."

"This isnae getting' us anywhere," Liam said then picked Mahri up and threw her over his shoulder.

"Malcolm," Liam snapped. "Bring those laddies tae th' castle."

The Transformation

Mahri put her lips in a tight line, determined not to say a word. Another woman might punch and scream, but she would do neither. When they got to the castle and she was back on the ground, he would hear quite a lot from her.

But to Mahri's frustration, it didn't quite happen that way. When they were near the stables, inside the castle, he dismounted in one smooth move then grabbed her by the waist and set her down. She looked up to see cold, hard eyes. He took a firm grip of her upper arm and walked quickly to the door.

Mahri tried to take in every room of the castle they walked through but he was walking too fast. She was turned around, losing her way. Mahri got distracted. The castle was warm and it was comfortable. She had never seen so many fires, or for that matter, fireplaces.

He kept walking, his strides impossible for Mahri to keep up with without running. His tight grip on her arm was sure to cause a bruise. They began taking stairs.

"Can ye please slow down? Ah am havin' difficulty keepin' up with ye."

Liam laughed again. "Dae ye think this is a tour of th' castle? Isnae."

"Ay course Ah dinnae think this is a tour of th' castle. Ah cannae keep up with ye."

Liam stopped in front of the door. "Nae need, we ur here."

He opened the door to a bedchamber the likes of which Mahri had never seen before. The bed looked like it was a cloud. It had some sort of padding under clean, comfortable looking blankets. Her body groaned for her to fall into that bed. Even though he had let her arm go, she didn't dare move. There was a fireplace and windows. There were two comfortable chairs next to the fireplace with a small table between them. There was a table against a wall with a looking glass on it and a seat below. Mahri had heard rumors of such a thing but she didn't believe them until now. There was a wardrobe. It was so large. No one could possibly have so many dresses that they needed such a large wardrobe.

He broke into her thoughts. "Ye will stay here. In th' morning, yer maid will bathe ye an' dress ye. Ye will stay here until I call ye for dinner. Is that understood?"

"Am Ah yer prisoner?"

He ran a hand through his hair in frustration, "Ah don't yet ken what Aam gonnae dae with ye. Until then, ye will be locked in here. Ah will see ye in the morrow evening."

Mahri could hear him put a key into the lock on the other side of the door. The final click of the bar made her flinch. She heard his footfalls grow fainter. She checked the door. Locked. Mahri sighed and turned around, leaning her back on the door.

The bed. She went and sat on the edge. "Ohhh," she never felt anything like it. She took off her shoes and got under the covers, fully clothed. This wasn't a social visit. She didn't have anything to change into.

Mahri woke the next morning feeling groggy. She sat up and rubbed her eyes then shook her head. She slept so well that her brain must have shut off. She hadn't heard the door unlock, nor had she heard the fire being built or the breakfast tray delivered. The smell of food cleared her mind.

"Hello," she called into the bedroom. No one seemed to be there now. She pulled the warm, soft covers aside and walked to see what food had been left on the table.

As far as she could remember, she never had food appear like that. For Mahri, every meal was a struggle. She stole, she trapped, she dug up kitchen gardens, and she rummaged through scraps thrown out the back door for the animals. She never had food appear to her before.

Porridge. How lucky was she? And it was still warm. Mahri sat in the chair next to the breakfast tray and ate. She dug into it with three fingers and sucked every bit of it from inside and the tips her fingers. She didn't waste any.

There was tea. Mahri had some, but she had never developed a taste for it. It was rare for her to have tea. What could she do? Boil water over a campfire every time she wanted a cup? How would she find tea leaves?

She was sipping her tea, lost in thought, wondering what had happened to her, when a servant knocked. Once Mahri beckoned her, she came in followed by two boys carrying a tub. Behind them, a line of boys carrying buckets of steaming water came to fill the tub.

A servant carried a small table over to the tub and placed it within reach. She placed the soap and a towel on top. Mahri's baths weren't more than a dunk in a cold loch. No soap, no hot water. "Over here, Miss," she said, beckoning Mahri to the tub. She helped Mahri out of her dress and undergarments, then left.

The water was a little hot but Mahri wouldn't wait another minute before getting in. She lay back and closed her eyes, her skin protesting the water temperature by turning red. Mahri tried to think when she last had a hot bath. It must've been years ago, when she was a girl.

A servant came back carrying an arm full of dresses in various colors. She put them on the bed and turned to help Mahri. She took a cloth and soaked it then washed Mahri's back. She took a cup, "Sit back, Miss, an' wet yer hair. Ah will wash it."

Mahri did as she was told. She gladly kept still as her hair was soaked. The whole time a servant was washing her hair, Mahri told her brain to remember the feeling of hot water cascading down her hair. She didn't know when she would ever have such a bath again. She wanted to remember the feel of fingers massaging her head. She closed her eyes.

"What is yer name?" Mahri asked.

"Dora," she said.

"Weel, Dora, thank ye for helpin' me. Ah havenae felt this good in a long time."

After Mahri's hair had dried by the fire, Dora handed her new underclothes to put on. Mahri took off her robe and donned the surprisingly well fitting garments. They had no stains or rips. Her underclothes looked to Mahri like they had never been worn before, they were so clean. Of course, they had, but Mahri would gladly enjoy the feel of the soft fabric against her skin.

"Will my own underclothes be clean an' sent back tae me in th' morrow? Ah don't want tae borrow these for tay long."

"Ah dinnae ken, Miss. Ah was told tae bring ye these clothes an' tae see if any ay them fit. Ye are tae try on each gown. All that fit are tae go in th' wardrobe," Dora said.

The first gown Mahri tried on was beautiful deep purple muslin with a deep purple ribbon at her waist. The neck was low and she pulled up the bodice every time she moved. Dora kept moving her hand away. Mahri had never seen anything so fine. It fit her well except it was a little short. The gowns owner must be shorter than Mahri.

As she stood there in the beautiful gown, body bathed, food given to her, fire in the fireplace, Mahri couldn't imagine anything better. She would remember this day when she next huddled in a stable on a wintry night trying to sleep.

Dora proclaimed all the gowns presentable. They weren't perfect. Either they were too tight or a bit too loose. Some were shorter than others were. Mahri thought them perfect. She told Dora she would wear the deep purple gown and the rest could go back. Dora ignored her and put the dresses in her wardrobe.

The lunch tray was sent to Mahri in her room. There was fruit, bread and cheese with a carafe of wine. She laughed when presented with the tray. Having a full belly and not having to keep an eye out for the danger of being caught taking something that wasn't hers made Mahri drowsy. Dora brought Mahri a nightrail and told her to rest. The Laird was expecting her at dinner.

Rest? In the middle of the day? Mahri didn't rest during the day. Ever. Where would she? In a barn? In the forest clearing? No. Only as a prisoner in a castle.

Dora returned at 5 o'clock to wake Mahri and dressed her for dinner. At 6 o'clock, a nervous Mahri went down to eat.

She stood at the entrance to the great hall looking at the mass of people seated at long trestle tables for the evening meal. She scanned the crowd for Liam, but did not find him. Then she remembered he was Laird and would be seated at the head table in the center seat.

When Mahri looked there, she saw nod at her then point to the empty seat to his left. He was so commanding, even when directing such a small thing as where she should sit. His eyes pierced hers then scanned her from head to foot and then back to her face, taking the task in a leisurely pace. She could have done the same, except it would be rude. His face looked as though it was carved from granite, it was so well defined and rugged.

His eyes were the deepest blue she had ever seen. When she looked into them, she imagined she could dive into them, so close to the color of a loch at night they were.

She hesitated, wondering why he arrested her for stealing bread then wanted her to sit at his side.

She reached him and curtsied, "Laird."

The story continues…

Amazon.com

Amazon.co.uk

Copyright Notice

Highland Dreams

By

Jamie MacSeaver

http://www.jamiemacseaver.com

http://www.beyondoriginal.com

PUBLISHED BY:

Beyond Original LLC and Jamie MacSeaver

Copyright © 2017 Beyond Original LLC, Jamie MacSeaver. All rights reserved.

No part of this publication may be copied, reproduced in any format, by any means, electronic or otherwise, without prior consent from the copyright owner and publisher of this book.

This is a work of fiction. All characters, names, places and events are the product of the author's imagination or used fictitiously.

_____

Printed in Great Britain
by Amazon